Lee Aucoin, *Creative Director*
Jamey Acosta, *Senior Editor*
Heidi Fiedler, *Editor*
Produced and designed by
Denise Ryan & Associates
Illustration © Susy Boyer
Rachelle Cracchiolo, *Publisher*

Teacher Created Materials

5301 Oceanus Drive
Huntington Beach, CA 92649-1030
http://www.tcmpub.com
Paperback: ISBN: 978-1-4333-5445-8
Library Binding: ISBN: 978-1-4807-1124-2
© 2014 Teacher Created Materials

Duck Pond Fun

wri... ...en

Illustrated by Susy Boyer

What is at the pond today?

There are four ducks swimming

4

three ducks diving

two ducks skiing

and one duck hiding.

11

Quack!